COLLEGE OF ALAMEDA LIBRARY

W9-CQK-790

PX
7
J6
D4
1989

Jones, S. D.
The debt.

WITHDRAWN

LENDING POLICY:
IF YOU DAMAGE OR LOSE LIBRARY MATERIALS,
THEN YOU WILL BE CHARGED FOR REPLACEMENT.
FAILURE TO PAY AFFECTS LIBRARY PRIVILEGES,
GRADES, TRANSCRIPTS, DIPLOMAS, AND REGISTRATION
PRIVILEGES OR ANY COMBINATION THEREOF.

MAR 17 2000
MAR 24 2000
MAR 27 2000
MAR 19 '97
MAR 14 '98

LENDING POLICY,
IF YOU DAMAGE OR LOSE LIBRARY
MATERIALS, THEN YOU WILL BE
CHARGED FOR REPLACEMENT. FAIL-
URE TO PAY AFFECTS LIBRARY
PRIVILEGES, GRADES, TRANSCRIPTS,
DIPLOMAS, AND REGISTRATION
PRIVILEGES OR ANY COMBINATION
THEREOF.

91

THE DEBT

AN AMERICAN FAMILY™ BOOK SIX: 1877

The Debt

S. D. JONES

FEARON EDUCATION
a division of
David S. Lake Publishers
Belmont, California

Cover illustrator: Nanette Biers

An American Family is a trademark of David S. Lake
Publishers. Copyright © 1989 by David S. Lake
Publishers, 500 Harbor Boulevard, Belmont, CA
94002. All rights reserved. No part of this book may
be reproduced by any means, transmitted, or trans-
lated into a machine language without written
permission from the publisher.

ISBN 0–8224–4756–8
Library of Congress Catalog Card Number: 88–81525
Printed in the United States of America
1. 9 8 7 6 5 4 3 2 1

Contents

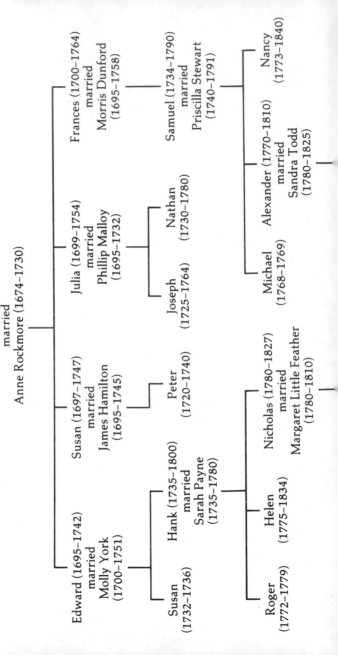

FAMILY TREE

Samuel Roberts (1672–1728)
married
Anne Rockmore (1674–1730)

Edward (1695–1742)
married
Molly York
(1700–1751)

Susan (1697–1747)
married
James Hamilton
(1695–1745)

Julia (1699–1754)
married
Phillip Malloy
(1695–1732)

Frances (1700–1764)
married
Morris Dunford
(1695–1758)

Samuel (1734–1790)
married
Priscilla Stewart
(1740–1791)

Susan
(1732–1736)

Hank (1735–1800)
married
Sarah Payne
(1735–1780)

Peter
(1720–1740)

Joseph
(1725–1764)

Nathan
(1730–1780)

Michael
(1768–1769)

Alexander (1770–1810)
married
Sandra Todd
(1780–1825)

Nancy
(1773–1840)

Roger
(1772–1779)

Helen
(1775–1834)

Nicholas (1780–1827)
married
Margaret Little Feather
(1780–1810)

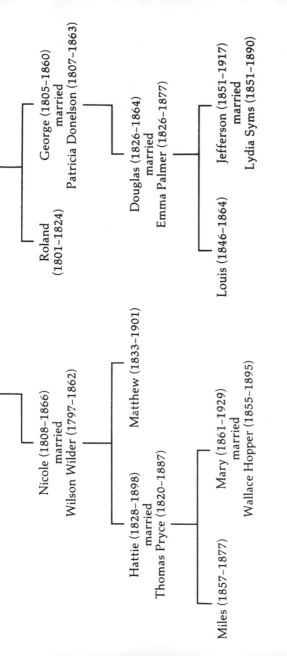

AN AMERICAN FAMILY™ SERIES

THE DEBT

CHAPTER 1

Message From a Stranger

"Oh, Mother," complained the girl standing on the pine-wood stool. "You're making me look just like a child. I don't want that silly old lace thing around my neck. I must have satin. Yards and yards of satin. Just like the debs of Columbia!"

"Mary Pryce stand still," her mother, Hattie, said. "You keep squirming and mouthing and I reckon I'll accidently jab you with this pin." She continued trying to straighten the hem of her daughter's skirt. She said, "You'll have your satin. But I'll vow you won't have 'yards and yards' of it. You'll look as modest and proper as a 16-year-old should.

Not like those big city women. South
Carolina has gone crazy since the war—and
the women along with it. They have no sense
of what's decent anymore."

Mary almost said something about this
being the 1870s and not the days of the
savages. But she knew that would only make
her mother angrier.

Hattie added, "Your father and Miles had
better get back from town soon. I have a
million chores and only two hands."

"Hah," said Mary. "You won't get help from
those two. Father thinks of very little but his
hunting these days. And Miles thinks of
nothing but the business. Ever since Daddy
made him an officer in his business, Miles
talks only of 'settling accounts.' The way he
carries on, you'd think everybody owes *him*
money. Even the Dunfords."

"The Dunfords *do* owe us money. That's
no secret."

"But they're our cousins!"

"Of course they are, dear. And that's why
your father's loans have been so large and his

terms so easy on them. He wants to help them rebuild their plantation."

"Exactly. They are *Daddy's* loans. Not Miles's. But it's always Miles who's so concerned about them."

"Your brother happens to be handy with numbers," Hattie replied.

"And little else."

"Mary Pryce, you watch your tongue."

"It's true, Mother. Suzanna Mills has taken a liking to him. But he doesn't even know she exists. I told her to replace that locket she wears with a bank key. Then Miles would surely take notice."

"You do talk nonsense sometimes, Mary Pryce." But Mary could not hear her mother through her own laughter.

Maybe Hattie's mind wandered. Or maybe she was just not thinking. But when she heard her daughter scream, she figured she had stuck her.

Hattie looked up at Mary and saw a look of horror on the girl's face. Mary screamed again. "It's just a pin, I could hardly have touched you!" But she saw that the girl's look of pain had nothing to do with the pin. She was staring at the doorway with a look of pure fright.

Hattie quickly turned to see what had so stunned Mary. The figure that stood in the shadow of the doorway was huge. It seemed to have no face, no features. If it had not made a motion with its walking stick, it would not have looked human.

"What do you want?" Hattie asked. Her voice showed no fear. "If you are a friend, show your face. You frighten my daughter."

"Sorry, ma'am," said the shadowy figure. The deep voice did nothing to calm the two women. "I didn't mean to scare you," the man said. He took a step back from the doorway and into the light of the backyard.

Now Hattie could see from his friendly expression that she had no cause for alarm. The man was indeed big shouldered and barrel-chested. He was black. Hattie judged him to be middle aged, although his snowy white hair made him look older. His modest clothes were clean and starched.

"Go away!" snapped Mary. Though she sounded angry, she was still very much afraid.

"Hush, child," ordered Hattie. "This man has done nothing but startle us." And to the man at the door she said, "I'm sorry we're so jumpy. We didn't hear you come to the door."

"I have news," said the black man.

"News?" exclaimed Hattie. "Is it my husband? Is Thomas all right?"

"I trust he is. No . . . no . . . I have news about your brother, Matthew."

"What?" said Hattie. She had not heard her brother's name uttered outside of her own prayers in more than five years. "Matthew? Is he alive? Where is he? How do you know him? Sit down and tell me everything."

The black man lowered his stooped frame into a straight back chair and smiled. It was a smile as warm as an evening fire. It made Hattie suddenly feel calm and relaxed.

"You seem just as Matthew described you," he said. "Full of life and love. My name is Rutlidge. I traveled for some time with your brother."

"I have some letters from him," Hattie said. "I can't recall anyone named Rutlidge. Though I don't doubt you. I haven't heard from my brother in more than a few years."

"Your brother is alive," said the man. "Did he ever mention in a letter a poor soul named Zeke?"

Hattie's eyes lit up. "Zeke! Yes, I remember the name. He did write of you."

"He saved my life more than once in the time I spent with him. I say he is alive and you can be sure of that. He wanted me to let you know that. But you would not recognize him if you were to meet him."

"Is he hurt or ill? Does he need help?" Mary asked of the uncle she had never seen.

"No," replied Zeke. "He does not need help. He is as independent a man as there ever was. Before the war I escaped from my masters. I traveled the underground from Tennessee out west. Your brother helped me to escape the men who tried to hunt me down. In the end, he too was hunted down for his efforts. But he proved a crafty fox and long ago outlasted the hounds. Thanks to the Indians who took him in."

"Indians!" Mary cried. "How did he come to live with Indians?"

Zeke said, "Most men live their lives not thinking, making no demands on life. Other men ask many questions and make many demands. These men get frustrated when their own society won't answer them back. Or when the answers make no sense, these men look elsewhere for reason. That was Matthew."

"What are you saying?" asked Hattie gently. "You said he is alive."

"He lives, yes ma'am. But not among white men. Not as a white man. The Indians took him in. The people of your mother and grandmother. He has lived with them, and as one of them, for the past 20 years."

"My lord," Hattie said. "How do you know this?" she asked. "How can you be sure?"

"After the Emancipation I made my way back from the west to my home in Memphis, Tennessee," Zeke said. "A family there sponsored my education. I was fortunate to have been sent to some fine schools. One was out west, where I met up again with Matthew." He took a letter from his pocket and handed it to her. "I wanted to prepare you. His writing has lost something of its former grace."

Hattie took the letter. The writing was rough, though the language was from the heart. It read, "Dearest Hattie, How often I think of you. And miss you. Everyday I pray you are happy. I am well. Do not worry. I have found my peace. How is Thomas? The children? You are everywhere with me. Matthew."

Hattie suddenly smiled and sat up straight. She was trying to shake herself out of the heartache she was feeling. How she had missed him. More than she remembered. "Well, Mr. Rutlidge. I hope you haven't come too far out of your way to bring word of my brother."

"No, ma'am. The truth is, I'm on my way to Charlotte to finish my law studies."

"You're a lawyer?" Mary asked in surprise.

"No, miss. Not yet. But I will be, I believe," Zeke replied. Then he sat back and smiled.

A Business Offer

A short while later Hattie heard a noise outside. Carriage wheels were grinding to a halt. A moment later Thomas Pryce walked in. "Supplies, food, sweets!" he said. "And . . . satin for my little girl."

"Oh, Daddy," cried Mary and ran to greet her father.

"Help your brother with the supplies," he told his daughter.

"This is my husband," Hattie said to Zeke.

Thomas stared at Zeke for a moment and then said, "Pardon me, sir, I had no idea my family had company." The tall, lanky man smiled and put out his hand. "The name is Thomas Pryce. I'm pleased to meet you."

"How do you do," said Zeke.

"This is Mr. Zeke Rutlidge," Hattie said. "He is a friend of Matthew's."

"Matthew?" said Thomas. "What word do you bring of him?" he asked with a worried look.

Zeke smiled and said, "Matthew is fine."

Hattie said, "Mr. Rutlidge was kind enough to bring us a letter from Matthew."

"A letter? Wonderful!" said Thomas. "It's good to finally know that Matthew is well. For that I'm thankful." Thomas went to the stove and poured himself a cup of tea. "Do you have other business in our fair town of Kettsborough, Mr. Rutlidge?"

"Mr. Rutlidge is studying law," said Hattie.

"Is he?" asked Thomas. "Well, Mr. Rutlidge, I admire you. The nature of law has always confused me. Any man who can make sense of it is to be congratulated."

Zeke smiled and said, "I'm not sure I have made sense of it. I think sometimes I'm too old for books."

"Nonsense!" said Thomas. "New worlds are opening up for the Negro. Your brothers need to see mature men leading the way. Not these young pups the Republicans are forcing on us. I know a lot of people don't share my views, but more's the pity."

"Yes, sir."

"Where are you staying?" asked Thomas.

"In Charlotte, sir," said Zeke.

"That's where the school is," added Hattie.

"Know anyone in the city?" asked Thomas.

"No sir, I don't. Only the one professor who recommended me."

"Well, that will never do. You're less than an hour's carriage ride from here. You'll have to promise us to spend the Sabbaths with us."

"Father!" Mary protested.

Even Hattie was a bit surprised at the offer. But she knew she shouldn't have been. Hattie was aware that her husband's heart had grown bigger and bigger every year they were married. Neither the war nor the South's defeat could deflate it.

Unlike many in the South—including the Dunfords—Thomas Pryce had seen the storm clouds of the Civil War forming. He knew the terrible effect war would have on the South and its people. So, before the full force of the war had begun to destroy the South, Thomas had shifted his business interests. And at war's end his businesses were fairly strong. Few businessmen in the South could claim as much.

Many people in town said Thomas's success was due to his business sense. Others complained that he was no better than a traitor to his own people. But Hattie knew that it was Thomas's heart—not his pocketbook—that kept him going.

"Thank you," said Zeke. "But I have no desire to impose upon you."

"Impose? Hardly, sir. Do not mistake my offer for kindness only. I am a businessman first and foremost . . ."

Even Mary had to smile at *that* statement. Thomas was a keen competitor true enough. But it was his son, Miles, who had managed the details of the business since he was 18.

"My son, Miles, is kept quite busy running my Charlotte concern. But I also have a dry goods operation here in Kettsborough. And it demands more time than either I or my son can give it. Here is my offer. Stay with us at the week's end and make sure the nuts and bolts of the business run smoothly."

"But . . ." Zeke protested.

"I can pay you very little. But the real-world business experience will do you good."

Zeke had longed to get involved in the actual day to day workings of business. Up to now he had always been barred from this world.

Even in 1877, most negroes could only get agricultural jobs. Though Zeke had studied hard, his books somehow took him farther away from what he saw as the real world.

"How could I refuse?" asked Zeke.

"You can't," laughed Thomas. "That's why I'm such a good businessman." Thomas patted Zeke on the back, and they shook hands to bind their agreement. "Hattie, show Zeke the rest of the house."

Hattie and Zeke disappeared into the living room. Thomas turned to see Mary marching in with a small pile of the lightest boxes she could find.

"I see I should have continued helping Miles myself," Thomas said frowning. "You're no help carrying things, I can see that. Now go and play hostess with your mother."

"Yes sir."

"Miles? How are you doing?" asked Thomas. He walked to the door and helped his son carry in the rest of their purchases.

"How's the leg?" Thomas asked Miles. It was a question Miles had often heard his father ask.

"It's fine—as usual. And I'm fine sir," Miles replied in a firm, clipped voice. He was sensitive about his right leg. It was smaller and shorter than his left leg. As a child, he was never able to do what other boys did— run, jump, play, fight. His short lean frame added to his frail look. But inside he felt as strong as any man, and he hated it when his father coddled him.

"Did you tell Mother?" Miles asked his father suddenly.

"No, I didn't. It was not the time."

"Mother will have to know sooner or later," Miles insisted. His sharp hawklike eyes glared at his father. "The Dunfords refuse to pay back three very large loans you made to them. That may result in the loss of one of our own business concerns," Miles said.

"They do not refuse. They cannot pay it back. They're your kin."

"Kin or not. You gave me the responsibility of setting the business straight. You are good at organization. But your books were, and continue to be, a source of trouble. Now I can only do so much, Father. As much as you let me. But I must tell you—"

Thomas quickly put his arm around his son. He held him lovingly but firmly, and looked the young man straight in the eyes. "Miles, you are the brightest star in the South as far as I'm concerned. You are only 20 and smarter than I ever was. You've helped me and my businesses in many ways. Pulled them out of ruin in some cases. And you know numbers like most people know the days of the week. But I'll tell you something. . . ."

Thomas sat the youth down and continued. "You know nothing about people! You saw the war through a little boy's eyes. The Dunfords run a plantation. They're landowners. And like most southerners who work the land they need time to recover. Not just from the war, but from the Republicans, the scalawags, and the carpetbaggers. The last thing they need is pressure from their southern brothers. I didn't get to where I am by being soft. But I never lost my soul for a dollar. Make sure you don't lose yours either, boy."

Thomas looked in his son's eyes. He hoped he saw a light shimmering deep inside them somewhere. But secretly he wondered whether the boy had already lost his soul to the dollar.

Thomas knew the look well. He had seen it in the eyes of a thousand different men—northern, southern, black, and white. It was a look of ambition without restraint, drive and determination without compassion. But he still hoped. He hoped that his son would reach inside himself and find a light.

Thomas patted Miles on the back and left to join the others.

Miles stayed behind. He thought about what his father had said. And the more he thought about it, the angrier he grew. Though no one else could hear, he said aloud in a snarl, "The Dunfords owe us, and the Dunfords will pay."

A Father's Fury

In the weeks that passed, Miles never gave another thought to his father's warning. Instead, the desire to extract payment from the Dunfords burned even stronger inside him.

Miles spoke little of it to his parents. Everyone thought his motives stemmed from a desire to set his father's business straight. But Miles knew the real reason for his attitude. And it devoured his peace of mind each waking moment.

As for Zeke, he continued to study law in Charlotte and visit the Pryces when he could. Though he was more than twice Miles's age, he became an eager student of the younger man.

Soon Zeke began to better understand the business world. He even saw himself one day as a great business leader. Zeke harbored many dreams—the kind that only men held in slavery can have. He read. He learned. He grew wiser each day.

Even Miles admired his student's drive. And he saw his association with Zeke as a way to better his own lot.

"I've met a group of Republicans through my father's business connections," Miles said to Zeke one day. "They operate from the state capital. They plan to groom me for a position of some importance there."

Zeke said, "I'm very happy for you."

"These gentlemen want to work with skilled and well-educated negroes such as yourself. I'll introduce you to them. I'd like to show them that I, too, as a southerner, share their ideals."

"Thank you, sir," said Zeke. He smiled as best he could. But he kept his true feelings to himself. Zeke knew that Miles was simply trying to use him to look good in the eyes of these Republicans.

Zeke also knew what the northern Republicans had been doing in the South since the Civil War. They were trying to drive a wedge between black and white men. They were using the black men as puppets. Zeke had little doubt that this is what Miles's sponsors in the capital would do as well.

"I need to prove to these men that I have what it takes," Miles said. "I have to show I can make any business run smoothly. And that means calling in all loans my father has made. Including loans to the Dunfords."

Just as Miles finished speaking, Jefferson Dunford burst through the office door. He was six years older than Miles. His hair was blond and fine, his jaw set and square. He was built like an athlete, strong and graceful.

Jefferson Dunford's teeth were clenched tightly. His eyes glared with anger. He held a piece of paper in a shaking hand.

"This is an insult to my father's name!" he cried. He walked past Zeke as though the man did not exist. "It's a good thing my father is dead. If he were alive, he'd tan your hide like the child you are."

"Well," said Miles calmly, "as you say, your father *is* dead. And my father is very much alive. So are his businesses and his debts."

"You know the problems I've had. The Yankees have all but ruined us. We need a few more years. We have to ride out the rule of these devilish radicals. We must have a chance to get on our feet again," Jefferson said.

Zeke stood and said, "I'd better go."

"No, stay," commanded Miles.

"Afraid to be alone with me, Miles?" Jefferson taunted.

But before Miles could reply, Zeke picked up his papers and left the room.

As the door closed Jefferson smiled and said, "I didn't think you believed in slaves anymore."

"Mr. Rutledge is a guest of this house," Miles replied.

"Is that what you call them now?" asked Jefferson. "Well I remember a time when the Pryce family *owned* guests like him—same as we all did. But you and your daddy turned your back on all that. Now you bow and scrape to them. Just like you bow and scrape to all the Yankees. You've turned your back on the South—"

"That's a lie."

"My daddy and my only brother were killed by the Yanks. Lots of good people, your neighbors, died trying to keep brats like you in silk britches. And this is how you repay us. Well you're worse than the Yankees. Your whole family is filled with traitors."

Miles grew angry. His face turned red and his body nearly shook with rage. Jefferson smiled and taunted him.

"Come on, Miles. Get real mad. Come after me. For once in your life—be a man."

Miles nearly forgot himself. He nearly forgot about his withered leg, and the differences in size and strength between him and his cousin. But he knew a fight would play right into Jefferson's hands. He took a deep breath and sighed.

"It seems that we're playing out some old scenes," Miles said.

"What?"

"You remember, Jefferson. Surely you remember how you and your brother used to tease me. Make fun of my leg . . . taunt me. Just like you're trying to do now. You'd bully me until I couldn't take any more. Then I always made the same mistake I was just about to make now. I'd go after you. And you'd whop me good. But now I don't need to do that. Because I can and will beat you where it counts—at the bank. I can bloody you so badly there, you'll never get up."

Jefferson Dunford stared at his cousin with a bewildered look on his face. Then he fell into a chair and sat there, stunned, as though he had been hit.

"You mean *that's* what all this is about? You'd ruin me, and my mother, and all that my family worked for, because we teased you?" He laughed heartily, but soon the laughter and the smile died. "You are one sad boy, Miles Pryce."

Miles then took a seat behind his desk. He took off the spectacles he wore whenever he worked and rubbed his eyes.

"You insult me more than you know, my cousin," said Miles. "It would be hard to believe a man could not rise above insults suffered as a child. No, Jefferson, that's not the reason."

"Then what?" snapped Jefferson.

Miles laughed. "You really don't have the slightest idea, do you? Of course not. It would be for your own peace of mind to forget. I'm sure you never think about that rainy winter during the war. I was just six then, and so was my little black friend, Joseph."

Jefferson had erased the name from his mind. But he spoke it now in a whisper, as though he dare not speak the name aloud. "Joseph."

"We were playing by the river bank," Miles went on. "We shouldn't have been, I know. The river was high that winter, and we'd been warned."

"You swore," snarled Jefferson. "You swore—"

"But the little slave boy, named Joseph, and I were playing by the river. Then some boys came along. I see your memory is coming back."

"Yes," said Jefferson, as if in a daze.

"And these boys began their usual taunts. As usual, I got angry and we all started to scuffle. Of course the fight was just between us. But, perhaps out of loyalty to me or out of fear for his own life, Joseph got in the way."

"Shut up."

"You pushed him—" Miles said.

"He fell!" Jefferson insisted.

"I saw you push him. And you laughed as he went beneath the rushing water. Everyone did. You had no problem swearing the others to secrecy. I was the only one who was outraged enough to tell. But you threatened me. You said you'd kill my mother and father if I ever told."

"We never would have. We were just kids."

"So was Joseph. But he never got to grow up to manhood. Afraid, and feeling guilty anyway, I took the blame. I told everyone that we were playing and Joseph had just slipped. Daddy whipped me, and I cried, and the slaves mourned. But it didn't last too long.

No one much cared. After all, he was just a little Negro boy. No one who mattered."

"Those were different times," Jefferson said.

"Joseph was my *only* friend. And I've lived with that secret eating away at me for years. As it will for the rest of my life. And never once in all the years have you said you were sorry."

Jefferson held his head in his hands. Now all the images came flooding back to him. And he saw in vivid horror the tragedy of that gray day.

"We were so young," he said. "So stupid then." He shook his head. But then he stopped and looked up at Miles, met his gaze. He stared at those deep, cold eyes as though he had just recalled another detail of the story. "But, remember this. The secrecy was a matter of honor."

"Honor?"

"Yes," said Jefferson. "Any one of us in our group would have done the same. You never tell on your friends. You never betray a fellow officer. For a true southerner it's simply a matter of honor. We were like one big brotherhood then. Still are. The war's done nothing to change that. Though the Yankees would like to think it has. And that's something *you* never understood. Not as a child and not now. You didn't fight in the war. You never knew what it was like. But honor is everything—sometimes even more than life."

Miles stared at Jefferson in disbelief. "You're not even sorry, are you?" Miles asked.

"Of course I'm sorry for what happened. But just one person was hurt. And that was a long time ago. What you're trying to do to me and my family is going to do far worse. You'll be putting dozens of negroes out of work. And you'll be destroying a little bit more of the South, too. Just what the Yankees have wanted all along. Is that really what you want?"

"You know," said Miles. "I always wondered what you'd say or do when I reminded you of that day. I wondered if you'd laugh or cry. But I never thought for one minute that you'd sink to talking about 'honor.' I never dreamed you'd be willing to brush off the whole sickening memory with talk of a southerner's honor. But it's better this way, really. If you had cried I might have forgiven you. And if you had laughed, I might have killed you. As it is, I'm just going to enjoy making you squirm. I'll go after every last penny you owe this family. Even if I have to bring everyone around you to their knees to do it."

Jefferson saw the fire in Miles's eyes. He knew the young man was determined to see the Dunfords destroyed. There was no use reasoning with Miles. It was clear that he was prepared to call in the loans. The Dunfords could lose their plantation.

Jefferson lowered his head sadly. "I'll see how quickly I can get you the money," he said. But he nearly choked on the words. He knew that there was no earthly way he could come up with that much cash.

As he turned to leave the room the door flew open. Thomas Pryce stood in the doorway. Though he appeared quiet and calm to Jefferson, Miles knew his father's look well. Thomas Pryce was boiling inside. He was nearly strangling himself with anger.

Thomas Pryce was typically a gentle and good-natured man. Very few people knew the rage of which he was capable. Miles had grown to fear little in life. But the look that crossed his father's face now brought chills down his spine.

Jefferson mustered as much of his manners as he could. "Good evening, sir," he said. "I was just leaving."

"Stay where you are, Jefferson," said Thomas. "I want you to hear what I have to say."

Jefferson stopped and took his seat. Miles sat back down behind his desk and waited for his father to speak. He could almost feel the anger before a word was uttered.

"As you know, Jefferson, at one time your father and I were partners. But it's been a while since I saw your mother. She's downstairs with Hattie now . . ." then he looked at Miles and added, ". . . in tears."

Thomas Pryce walked toward Miles clutching a paper in his hands. Suddenly he flung the paper on the desk in front of Miles. "Emma is crying because she's not able to repay the loans I made to your family these past years."

"Your son and I have just been . . . discussing the matter," said Jefferson. "If I could just—"

Thomas Pryce put up his hand to stop him. "The piece of paper I have laid before my son is the agreement your mother and I signed." Thomas picked up the paper and held it high. Then he ripped it.

First he tore it in half, then in half again. And he tore it one last time until the pieces of the document fell to the floor.

"Father! What in the world are you doing?" Miles cried. He could not believe what he had seen. Was his father serious? Was he crazy?

"As of this day, I cancel all debts owed to me by the Dunfords," Thomas declared. "My only regret, Jefferson, is that I did not do this sooner."

Neither Jefferson nor Miles could believe their ears. Jefferson froze, unable to utter a word of the joy he felt.

Miles was furious. He was shaking as he said, "Father that decision is no longer yours to make. You gave me complete power—"

But Thomas cut him off in midsentence. "You have whatever power I decide to give you. I can give it and I can take it away."

Miles grew weak with anger and frustration. His knees started to buckle and he felt faint. He had waited so long to put Jefferson Dunford in his place. He had lived through years of silent agony just waiting for one day. And that was the day he'd make Jefferson and his family pay for the harm they had caused him.

Now the battle was all over before a single shot had been fired. Once more Jefferson would walk away in triumph. And once more Miles would suffer utter defeat.

Miles knew there was no use arguing with his father. When Thomas Pryce made up his mind about something, nothing and no one could change it.

"Now I've said my piece," Thomas added. "I know there's a wall between you two men, though I cannot say why. But if you ask my advice, it's time to tear that wall down. Shake hands like two southern gentlemen and forget about this whole matter. But whether you choose to or not, it is none of my affair." And with that, Thomas shook Jefferson's hand and walked out.

Jefferson extended his hand for Miles to take. But Miles turned away and spoke in a cold, menacing whisper. "Don't think for one minute this is over. It's just begun. As far as I'm concerned you have yet to pay. And I *will* make you pay . . . in full."

A Desperate Plan

With each pasing day, Miles's anger and frustration grew. He could only watch as his father stripped away more and more of his power. He watched as Jefferson tried to rebuild his fortunes. And though his cousin did not possess Miles's business sense, the plantation managed to survive.

It seemed to Miles that his whole family was against him. He had told himself that he had badgered Jefferson for the good of his father, mother, and sister. They were just too blind to see it, he told himself.

A month later, Miles sat in his office deciding what his next move would be. He tried to ignore the anger of his father. He tried not to notice the disappointment of his mother. And he never once abandoned his desire to destroy Jefferson.

He was pacing his office when his mother entered.

"Hello, Miles," she said. "Mary and I were shopping. I thought I'd stop by to see you. Mary is still trying on hats. I know I must be disturbing—"

"No," Miles replied bitterly. "Come in. I'm quite free, as a matter of fact. Father has seen to it that I have less and less to do. He no longer trusts me."

"He *does* still trust you. And he loves you deeply. That's what I came to talk to you about."

"Then why has he taken my power away? Doesn't he know he's ruining my chances with the Republicans?"

"Your feelings against Jefferson . . ."

"What of them?"

"They run so deep. Your father is afraid you'll do something foolish and—"

"Embarrass the business?" Miles asked.

"No. Not that. He simply wants to remind you that there is more to business than money."

"So this is his punishment? To humiliate me in front of Jefferson?"

"Jefferson is only a—"

"Jefferson Dunford is a thief," Miles said coldly.

"I'll not have you talk that way. You have to remember that Jefferson is your cousin. He's one of the family. And since his father died, he's like a son to your father and me."

"A son?" Miles cried. The very thought sickened him.

"Not like you, of course," Hattie said. "You'll always be our very own. But Jefferson is important, too. Our roots with the Dunford family run deep. And there is something else . . ."

"What is it?"

"You should know that we have decided to do more to help the Dunfords make the plantation work."

"Do more?" exploded Miles. "What more can you do? You've already cancelled all their debts."

"We thought Mr. Rutlidge could lend a hand—"

"Rutlidge?" Miles could not believe his ears. "Zeke Rutlidge is *mine*. Father has put him under my own guidance. He can help our business."

"But that's just it. You run things so well. You don't need Zeke. And Jefferson does *not* have your business sense. He could use a man like Zeke to organize—"

"I won't hear of it. This is the last straw, Mother! You and Father have done everything you can to work against me. It's one thing to let the Dunfords struggle on their own. But it's quite another to actually give them our own money and men."

Hattie scowled. It was not often that she grew angry. But Miles's stubborn attitude was more than she could stand. "I'm sorry you feel that way, Miles. I was hoping you might show a little compassion."

"What does compassion have to do with it? You've all let that war soften you. I'm too young to remember it, and I'm glad. Because I can see things clearly. I want to make this family great, and make the South a force again. But you and Father, and everyone else, still live by the old code. Your vision is clouded with sentiment and *compassion*. Can't you understand that that way of life is dead? The old South lies under the ruins of Atlanta."

"Don't you talk like that," Hattie said angrily.

"Why don't you just go ahead and employ Jefferson *here*? Give him my job. One son is as good as another."

"Are those the words of a man with clear vision?" Hattie asked. "You're talking nonsense. I'll leave. I can see you are still in no mood to think straight. But I hope that when you calm down, you'll see there's reason to all this. Jefferson is *family*!"

Hattie stormed out the door leaving Miles furious.

Has everyone gone mad? Miles wondered. How could they call his mortal enemy "family"? How could his own mother do this to him? How could his parents betray him?

Miles cried out in rage and pounded his fist against the wall. "I'll see you burn before I call you 'family,' Jefferson Dunford!"

Miles sat down at his desk to gather his thoughts. It all seemed very clear to him. All of his power was being taken away. Much of his family's money was being drained by the ungrateful Jefferson. And now his parents spoke of his cousin as a son! They spoke of Jefferson with pity and love. But they seemed to speak of Miles with disappointment and regret. Miles felt abandoned.

He tried to calm himself. But the moments of calm did not change his feelings. They only served to strengthen them. He would put an end to the Dunford problem once and for all. He made up his mind that day. Severe measures would have to be taken. And taken now!

Miles began planning the Dunfords' downfall that same afternoon. He knew that Jefferson would never agree to let a man like Zeke help run his plantation. He knew that his parents' plan to help Jefferson would never work.

So what would their next plan be? Would they make him another loan? Would they take Jefferson and his mother into the house?

Would his father set Jefferson up in business? If Jefferson rejected Zeke, all of these nightmares were possible. But Miles vowed to himself that these would never take place.

Miles needed to hear for himself what had happened at Zeke's meeting with Jefferson. That night, he picked Zeke up and invited him to dinner at the Briarwood Inn.

The Briarwood was the town's oldest inn. At one time it was nestled in an out-of-the-way spot amid rolling hills and old oaks. But after the war, buildings rose up around it. Now, no more than a few blocks away, the poor had raised their shanties. Men, both black and white, stood about all day with very little to do. And violence was as near, and as sudden, as a summer storm.

Only a few days before a black man had been pulled from a ditch in the road and lynched. He had become another victim of the outlawed Ku Klux Klan. That secret and violent brotherhood represented either the hopes or the fears of all southerners.

The Klan was committed to terrorizing the black man. And it was intent on establishing the power of the South once more. The Klan soothed the feverish brow of the bitter and the defeated. But it was also a nightmare to a lot of southerners. For there were many people who wanted to awake to a new day and put the war behind them.

The Briarwood Inn itself had not changed. It continued to cater to the more well-to-do people in the area. And the owners had stopped snubbing the Yankees long ago. Their need for money far outweighed any social or political concerns.

Miles and Zeke sat near a window and watched the sun set behind the hills to the west.

"Tell me everything, Zeke," said Miles through a mouthful of bread. "What did he do?"

"Well," said Zeke, "I told Jefferson that Mr. Thomas Pryce thought I could be of help in running things. Not take over the day to day management of the plantation or anything like that. But maybe I could help with the distribution of the cotton, and finding buyers, that sort of thing."

Miles laughed heartily. "I'm sorry for laughing, Zeke," he said. "But I would have loved to have been there. Just to see the look on Jefferson's face when you told him *you* were sent to help *him*!"

Zeke stiffened and said, "Master Dunford did not take kindly to the offer. And he told me so. He said that 'my kind' was meant to work the land—not buy and sell it. And that it would be a cold day down below before I would tell him what to do. I tried to tell him that I looked on it as a favor to *me*. To help me get the experience I needed in the world. But he wanted none of it."

Miles tried hard not to laugh. But he couldn't help himself. Imagine! A former slave offering his skill to a fine southern gentleman as Jefferson Dunford!

"Why do you think it's funny?" asked Zeke angrily. "I'm getting too old for this. There are Negroes half my age and twice as defeated. They're not able to read, threatened if they vote, beaten if they vote wrong. I feel like an old leaf—blown here by the northern wind and there by southern wind. Folks think they're being helpful. But I don't know if that's true. Well, I've had enough. I'd best ride back to town. Will you be coming with me?"

"No," Miles replied. "You go on ahead. I want to have another helping of this bread and coffee."

But Miles had more on his mind than food. "So, their plan failed," he said to himself. "Soon I'll be hearing more talk of favors to the Dunfords. But they'll need more than favors to help them now."

It was dark when Miles finally left the inn. But he did not turn east toward his home or the homes of Kettsborough's other wealthy people. Instead he turned west. He walked toward the filthy row of shanties near the river.

Miles's small well-dressed figure made a comical sight in the shantytown. He was quickly spotted, but that did not bother him. Miles wanted to be noticed. He wanted to be noticed by one man in particular. He was a black man with a silver head of hair, and muscles like iron. And he always carried a gold-colored walking stick that he sometimes used as a club.

This man had been pointed out to Miles days earlier. A fellow businessman claimed that this black man would perform any service for a fee. And he didn't care how dangerous—or deadly—it was.

As Miles had suspected, the man was not hard to find. He stood apart from many of the other poor people who always gathered in small groups in the shantytown. And his large frame and silver hair made it impossible to mistake him for anyone else.

"What is your name?" Miles asked.

"Jud," said the black man.

Miles silently handed the man a large pile of cash. The man counted it and then looked up at Miles.

"What do you want?" he asked.

Miles asked the man to come closer. In the darkness of the man's old shack, Miles laid out his plans. The black man with the gold cane did not react. He had heard it all before.

Many of the people in the shantytown stood just outside the door of the shack. They were hoping to see a fight or hear a bit of a rumor. But the brief meeting ended, and the people walked away disappointed.

None of them knew what Miles had said to the man called Jud. Three full days passed before any of them discovered a thing.

Then on the fourth day, loud cries came from the small, poor community. "Fire! There's been a fire!"

"The Dunfords' plantation. Five acres have been destroyed. Part of the house too. And somebody was killed."

"How'd it happen?" someone asked.

"Weren't no accident, that's for certain. Someone liquored up the workers. Fights started. Next thing, the place is up in flames."

The cries of "fire" carried clearly through the night air. The people eating at the Briarwood Inn could hear the people shouting. It sounded almost like a celebration.

But for Miles Pryce sitting at the inn by himself, there was no reason to celebrate. He simply rose, shut the window nearest his table, and sat down again. He already knew what had happened.

Miles stared sadly into his drink. What had gone wrong? There was supposed to be a fire. But fire to destroy the *crops*. No one was supposed to get hurt. There weren't supposed to be any fights. Only the crops were to burn. *Not the house!*

Even with the window closed Miles could still hear the people yelling. And the voices outside mixed with those in his mind. He tried to block out the sounds in his head, but he could not. He kept hearing the voice of an old woman crying out, "Fire! Fire!"

No matter what he did he could not shut that voice from his head. No one was supposed to die. *No one.* He hated Jefferson, that was true. But he had nothing against Emma Dunford, Jefferson's mother.

Emma was old. She could not move easily. By all the reports, a burning beam had fallen on her. Oh, dear God, thought Miles, what have I done? *I've killed her. I've killed her.*

Miles's conscience was filled with guilt. But he needn't have worried about anyone thinking that he was involved. No one in town or in his family suspected his part in the tragedy. After all, Miles was nowhere near the plantation on the night of the fire. Many folks suspected a tall black man. He had been seen nearby right before the fire had started. Some people said he was probably liquored up and not in his right head. It wouldn't be the first time something like that had happened.

Stirring Up Trouble

A man in overalls sat on the steps of the Dunford's house. His hair was wild—like his eyes. A red handkerchief hung from the back of his pants pocket. He chewed on a piece of hay and watched the end of it twirl around in front of his nose.

But when the people started to arrive, he stopped chewing. Instead, he stared rudely at each one of the people who had come to pay their respects.

Most of the house was still standing. Only the parlor and the back sun porch had been destroyed.

Thomas and Hattie Pryce made their way up to the front steps. Miles and his sister

Mary followed. The man in the overalls did not move right away.

"Excuse us," said Thomas Pryce.

The man smiled up at Thomas stupidly as though he did not understand. Thomas was about to repeat his request. Just then, the man lifted his two legs slowly out of the way. "Evening," he drawled.

Once inside, they saw her. Jefferson's mother, Emma Dunford, was lying in a coffin in the living room. Neighbors and friends were quietly talking.

Some of the women were weeping. Many of the men were off in the dining area. Several shook their heads and said that the North was to blame. Others said that negroes could not handle their new found freedom. Many men agreed with this. A black man had been seen starting the fire. But no one had caught him. And no one knew for certain who it was.

"Where's Jefferson?" Mary asked her mother.

"I don't know," Hattie replied. "I wouldn't be surprised if we see little of him tonight. He and his mother were very close. He's very upset."

Thomas said, "Emma was all Jefferson had left in the world. His father and brother died in the war. We're his only family now." Thomas had raised his voice a little so that Miles could hear. Miles was standing alone and apart from the others.

Hattie scolded her husband for his anger. "He's sorry. Just look at him."

Everyone guessed why Miles looked so pale and somewhat guilty tonight. It was no secret that Miles had pressured the Dunfords to repay their loans. Everyone thought Miles felt guilty for having treated the old woman's family so badly. They could not know that Miles felt guilty for having caused Emma's death. He felt just as responsible as if he'd set the fire himself.

"Have you seen Jefferson?" Hattie asked her son.

"No, Mamma," was all Miles said.

In fact, no one had seen Jefferson for hours. Earlier, as the number of guests had increased, Jefferson felt he could no longer bear up. He had left to walk around his property—to be by himself.

Jefferson loved to walk the dirt roads that skirted his father's land. He loved the rich soil and the sweet smell of the grass. And the rustling of the trees in the wind always made him feel better.

But today he felt numbed to the magic of the land. His heart was filled with rage and confusion. How could this all have happened? Who was responsible? He vowed to find out.

As he walked on, a man blocked his way. It was the man in the overalls with the red handkerchief.

Once again he was chewing on a piece of hay. He grabbed the handkerchief from his pocket and dabbed his brow. He smiled at Jefferson. Jefferson stared back.

"Howdy Jeff," the man said.

"Hello Roscoe," said Jefferson.

"Shouldn't you be back at the house with the other mourners?" asked Roscoe.

"I suppose I should," said Jefferson. "But I can't face them now. I think Mamma would understand."

"I reckon she would," said Roscoe. He scooped up a handful of dirt and let it fall through his fingers. "Pretty soil. Any idea why things aren't going your way?"

"I have some ideas," said Jefferson.

"Shoot," laughed Roscoe. "I'll just bet you do. Yankees came down and ruined this land. Freed slaves don't want to work the land. But they don't know what else to do.

"It's not just them," Roscoe went on. "It's Miles Pryce and his family. Taking all the money they've been making off their southern brothers and investing it up north. That's right. It's not just the Negroes. It's the whole thing. The whole thing stinks."

"You fixing to make a point, Roscoe?" asked Jefferson.

"Join up with us, Jeff. Join up with the Klan," Roscoe urged him.

"Klan's outlawed, you know that."

"Yep. I know that," Roscoe said. "They outlawed burning houses and killing women, too, near as I remember. But that don't stop some folks. Look, Jeff, how long have we been friends? Since we were kids. I know you.

With someone like you in the Klan, we'd be unbeatable! And I know you feel the same as me about the darkies."

"I'm not as proud of it as you seem to be."

"You bet I'm proud. Proud to be from this state and this part of the country. And with the Klan leading the way, we can bring the South back to its glory. To the way things used to be before the war."

Jefferson shook his head. "No, it's over."

"It ain't over!" Roscoe shouted.

"Take a look around!" said Jefferson. "You think the Klan can change what's happening? You think they can do what the whole force of Jeff Davis's army couldn't?"

"I do," Roscoe said firmly.

"Then you're crazy. The whole economy is changing, Roscoe. The whole way of life here. You see it every day. Heck, the Pryce's even sent their man Rutledge by to help *me* run my own business!"

"That's because they *want* your business. That's no secret."

"Only Miles wants it," Jefferson said. "For revenge."

"So, and who's always hanging around Miles? That Negro, Rutlidge. And who was seen starting the fire? A big old Negro with white hair."

"You'd better be sure before you say things like that," Jefferson warned him.

"Well, who else could it be? One day they send him to try to horn in on things. And the next day they burn your place to the ground—kill your mamma. And you wonder who did it? I don't know how you can stand it, boy! I'd be raising the Confederate flag and letting out hollers that'd make every northerner's blood freeze."

Jefferson lowered his head and tears came into his eyes.

"I feel the same way you do," he said. "God, I do. I wish someone would rid me of Miles Pryce and that puppy of his—Rutlidge. I wish they'd *all* disappear. But they won't. The South belongs to them now. I'm finished. This plantation's finished."

Jefferson Dunford started to cry. He fell to his knees and wept bitterly. How he hated everyone and everything.

Roscoe knelt beside him and whispered, "You ain't finished, Jefferson. The South ain't finished. And I'm going to prove it to you. I'm your friend. We got to stick together."

Jefferson looked into Roscoe's face. The man had a fiery look in his eyes. His mouth was twisted and his jaw was set. He looked like a person just itching to fight someone.

Jefferson just shook his head. "There's nothing you—we—can do about the way things are now, Roscoe. I wish there *was* something we could do. But there isn't."

Roscoe stood and backed away. "I'll prove it to you, Jeff. I swear it. You'll see! I'll get even for you."

As the man in the overalls ran down the dirt road, his voice faded away. Jefferson sat alongside the road, unable to get up enough strength to stand. He wondered what Roscoe was talking about.

"Get even for me?" asked Jefferson aloud. "What in the world . . ." He never did know what the fellow was talking about. He wondered whether Roscoe himself knew half the time.

But Roscoe did know. He knew what he had to do to prove to his friend that all was not lost. He raced to his old shack and grabbed his hunting rifle.

"I'll show them all!" Roscoe yelled. He put on his old gray cap, the one he'd worn in the battle at Ryker's Hill. He looked at himself proudly. He'd change things in this town even if he had to do it single-handedly. But he knew he wouldn't have to do it alone. He knew there would be plenty of men to help him.

Ambush

The wake had been simple and short. Jefferson finally appeared just as the preacher was offering up a last prayer for Emma.

The evening wore on and all the guests finally went home. Despite his mother's protests, Miles decided to accompany Zeke to a Republican rally that night.

Hattie had said it would not look right if Miles were to go to such an affair. What Zeke did was his own business. But out of respect for Emma, Miles should spend the evening quietly at home. It would only be proper.

But Miles could not sit still. He was racked with pain and guilt over the death of Jefferson's mother. He had to get out.

It was an unusually cool September evening. The political rally was loud and enthusiastic. The speakers promised more reforms, more jobs, better times. It was just the same old thing for Miles. But for Zeke it was a kind of dream.

Zeke listened to two black politicians speaking about their lives. And he realized for the first time in his life that he was capable of doing the same thing. He could become a leader—not only of his people, but of all people. Yes, he was old. Yes, it would take time and study. Yes, the odds were against him. But he truly believed he could do it.

After the rally, Miles and Zeke began the ride home. "I just might run for office someday, Miles," Zeke said.

Miles smiled. "I don't see why not. I'll bet with my connections, I just might be able to help."

Zeke shook his head. He could not possibly expect a man like Miles to understand. Miles had been given everything from birth. How could he understand how some people need to succeed on their own. But that changed nothing. Zeke vowed to himself that before he died, he'd make something of himself.

The night was cool and calm. Along this road, travelers could often hear animals stirring in the woods. So neither Miles nor Zeke took notice of the sounds coming from both sides of the trail.

Then suddenly, without warning, three horsemen exploded from the woods. They cut off both men's horses in midgallop and forced Miles and Zeke to pull them up.

Quickly sensing danger, Miles and Zeke turned to ride off in the other direction. But as they did, three more horsemen leapt into their path, blocking their way.

Zeke's blood turned cold. His eyes stared in terror at the men surrounding him. Each rider's face was covered by a large gray mask. The rest of their gear was dark-colored. One man wore a red handkerchief over his mouth and nose. Zeke realized he was looking at members of the Ku Klux Klan.

Zeke had been in tight places before. He'd been out West with Hattie's brother, Matthew, on the run from bounty hunters. But this was different. There was no way out. And Zeke knew it.

Miles reached inside his coat pocket. But the man with the red handkerchief aimed his rifle.

"Don't do it!" the man shouted. "We got nothing against you, sir. You can ride on. It's him we want." He waved his rifle at Zeke.

Neither Zeke nor Miles recognized that the masked man was Roscoe Lee, Jefferson's friend.

"Zeke's done nothing to you," said Miles. "Let him be. Your fight is with me."

"Oh? Ask this man who burned down the Dunfords' place," Roscoe shouted. "Ask him who killed Emma Dunford. He did! And he's going to pay!"

The other men echoed their agreement, letting out loud whoops and war cries.

"It wasn't Zeke," Miles said. "I swear it!"

Roscoe said, "Hear that, men? He's even sticking up for the boy. Well, let me tell you, Miles Pryce. A lot of folks saw a big old Negro boy with white hair set fire to the Dunford place. And everyone knows Jefferson just about threw your friend here right out of the house."

Miles could not think fast enough. How could he tell them that it was *he* who had paid to have the fire set? How could he convince them that another man—not Zeke—was responsible.

Miles thought of a hundred things to say. But all the words got jumbled up with his fear. He saw the man in the red handkerchief take aim at Zeke. And all Miles could think of was to set things right. He could not let Zeke die to save his own skin.

Just as Roscoe was about to pull the trigger, Miles drew his pistol.

Zeke shouted, "No!"

Miles fumbled with the weapon.

Roscoe spied Miles's pistol and fired.

A terrible, loud shot rang through the woods. Miles slumped forward and fell from his horse.

"Let's get out of here," someone shouted.

"Yeah, come on, Roscoe. Let's scoot."

Roscoe was wild-eyed with fear and hate. He stared at Miles's writhing body. "All right," he said. "But first let's do the job we came to do." He raised his rifle and aimed it at Zeke's chest. The black man closed his eyes and offered up a prayer.

A Sad Mother's Letter

Miles Pryce felt the life slowly draining from him. He rolled over, trying to free his arm. "Someone must have heard the shots," he murmured. "Someone . . ." He grabbed hold of his gun and fired two more shots into the air. He listened as the wind carried the sounds of the shots. They seemed to take flight, like birds exploding from a nest.

"Someone . . . please . . . oh God . . . forgive me . . . ," Miles whispered. He stared up at the cold night sky. How did all this happen? he asked. How could he have let things go this far?

He wished he could help Zeke. He wished he could go back in time and start over. He would act differently, he swore. He would help the Dunfords. He would help Jefferson. If only he could have another chance. He closed his eyes and prayed for help.

Help came but not soon enough to save Miles Pryce. All they could give him was a better place to die. His last moments were spent in his own house. His mother, father, and sister stayed close by to comfort him.

Miles was able to confess to his parents what he'd done. But it was not the confession that eased his mind. It was not those few feeble words that released him from his guilt. Nor was it his parents' forgiveness. It was not these things that comforted Miles in his last living moments. It was the sight of his family, together. It was the feel of their hands in his. For so long he had felt like an outsider. Now he realized that he had always belonged.

Once he tried to sit up, but his father stopped him. "Take it easy, son," he said. "Just rest."

"Is Zeke all right?" Miles asked.

"You don't have to worry about him," was all Thomas said.

Thomas knew it would do no good to tell Miles the truth. He could not tell him that they found Zeke just a few yards from where Miles had fallen. The black man had managed to crawl a short distance after he, too, had been shot. But he had bled to death in a ditch by the side of the road.

"They found the men who did this," Hattie said. "Jefferson led the lawmen to them. He had an idea of who it might be."

"Jefferson." Once more that word sprung with affection from his mother's lips. But now the sound of it did not anger Miles. All the petty hatred, all the years of bitterness seemed to melt away. They meant nothing to him now. All that mattered was his family.

"Tell Jefferson I'm sorry," said Miles.

Hattie nodded her head. "He knows, son," she said.

"We love you, Miles," said Mary.

His young sister tried to hold back her tears, but not out of bravery. She simply had a hundred more things she wanted to tell Miles. Little things, comforting things. But she never got the chance.

Miles Pryce closed his eyes and died.

Hattie and Mary started to cry. Thomas put his arms around them and held them. And then he broke down and wept, too.

As the days passed Hattie wondered how such a tragedy could have happened. She blamed herself. She blamed the war. The memory of her son's violent death continued to haunt her. But the thought of her brother—whom she long ago had given up for dead—gave her strength.

She liked to think of her brother, dressed in a chief's robes, looking over some great plain. And, she hoped it would be a land of peace—one with no war or violence.

Hattie walked into her bedroom and sat for a moment. She breathed deeply. Then she reached into her drawer and removed a piece of paper and a pen. She began to write to the brother she had not seen in nearly 25 years.

"Dear Matthew, I nearly wept when your friend Zeke told me you were still alive. How I long for the days when you and I, and Mamma and Pa, sat by the fire at home. Remember how Mamma would sing songs? Remember how Pa would tell stories? I hope you do those things with your loved ones now. I no longer do. Life here has grown bitter in recent years. We had such grand days before the war. Now everyone struggles to stay alive. And some do not make it . . ."

Hattie set down her pen. She had not meant the letter to take such a sad turn. She had wanted to speak of the faith she had in her family. She had wanted to say something about Jefferson. She was going to tell him about Miles—and about Zeke. But she thought better of it. The news would only sadden Matthew. Instead, she dug deep within herself and tried to find some happiness.

"Still, through it all," she wrote, "I believe we can be whole again. That one day we won't talk about North versus South. One day we will truly be one nation—one people—one family . . ."

There was no use writing more. She could not mail the letter. How could she? She did not know where her brother was. She slipped the letter back into her desk.

Maybe she would finish it when she was feeling better. And maybe she would find Matthew again one day. Maybe.

Hattie Pryce clung to the hope, and it made her feel better. It gave her the strength to lay her son to rest. To lay the bitter struggles of her kin to rest. And to go on.

2450